For Kathie Berlin, who loves swimming
and a good laugh—NK

For Auntie Carm—a continuing inspiration in
her 99th year—AB

GROSSET & DUNLAP
Published by the Penguin Group
Penguin Group (USA) Inc., 375 Hudson Street, New York,
New York 10014, USA
Penguin Group (Canada), 90 Eglinton Avenue East, Suite 700,
Toronto, Ontario M4P 2Y3, Canada
(a division of Pearson Penguin Canada Inc.)
Penguin Books Ltd., 80 Strand, London WC2R 0RL, England
Penguin Group Ireland, 25 St. Stephen's Green, Dublin 2, Ireland
(a division of Penguin Books Ltd.)
Penguin Group (Australia), 250 Camberwell Road, Camberwell,
Victoria 3124, Australia
(a division of Pearson Australia Group Pty. Ltd.)
Penguin Books India Pvt. Ltd., 11 Community Centre, Panchsheel Park,
New Delhi—110 017, India
Penguin Group (NZ), 67 Apollo Drive, Rosedale,
Auckland 0632, New Zealand
(a division of Pearson New Zealand Ltd.)
Penguin Books (South Africa) (Pty.) Ltd., 24 Sturdee Avenue,
Rosebank, Johannesburg 2196, South Africa

Penguin Books Ltd., Registered Offices:
80 Strand, London WC2R 0RL, England

Library of Congress Control Number: 2010040830

ISBN 978-0-448-45570-9   10 9 8 7 6 5 4

George Brown, CLASS CLOWN

Wet and Wild!

by Nancy Krulik

illustrated by Aaron Blecha

Grosset & Dunlap
An Imprint of Penguin Group (USA) Inc.

Chapter 1

George Brown stared at his computer screen. Louie had invited him to his birthday party. That was weird. *Really* weird. Because Louie *hated* George

From George's very first day at Edith B. Sugarman Elementary School, Louie had let him know that **they were never going to be friends** . . . *ever.* Louie still sometimes

called George **"New Kid"**—like he couldn't be bothered remembering George's real name.

Louie had also gotten George in trouble with the cafeteria lady—the *big, scary* cafeteria lady—just for **sneezing** in the middle of lunch. Apparently Louie didn't like snot anywhere near his food. He'd also thrown George out of a rock band for no reason except that he could.

No doubt about it, Louie *really* didn't like George. And George *really* didn't like Louie, either. **So they were even**.

Of course, that didn't mean George was

going to miss Louie's party. George might not have liked Louie, but he sure liked water parks.

George didn't want to give Louie a chance to take back his invitation, so he quickly typed an e-mail back saying that he would come.

I'll be at your party. Thanks for inviting me.

—George

George didn't even have time to blink before **a new e-mail flashed on his screen**. It was from Louie.

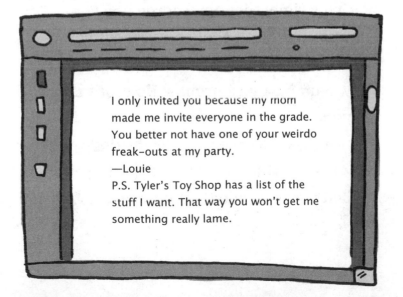

I only invited you because my mom made me invite everyone in the grade. You better not have one of your weirdo freak-outs at my party.
—Louie
P.S. Tyler's Toy Shop has a list of the stuff I want. That way you won't get me something really lame.

Oh brother. *Louie* was the lame one. Still, George understood what Louie meant by "weirdo freak-outs." George *had* been doing a lot of really strange stuff ever since he moved to Beaver Brook.

But it wasn't really his fault. **It was the super burp's fault.**

It had all started on George's first day at Edith B. Sugarman Elementary School. George's family had moved—again. That meant George was the new kid—**again**.

This time, though, George had promised himself that things were going to be different. He was turning over a new leaf. No more pranks. **No more class clown.**

But new George was also **boring George**. At the end of that first day, nobody even seemed to know he existed.

4

It was like he was *invisible* George.

That night, George's parents took him out for dessert to cheer him up. While they were sitting outside at the ice cream parlor and George was finishing his root beer float, **a shooting star flashed across the sky**. So George made a wish:

I want to make kids laugh—but not get into trouble.

Unfortunately, the star was gone before George could finish the wish. So **only part of it** came true—the first part, about making kids laugh.

A minute later, **George had a funny feeling in his belly**. At first he thought it was because of the root beer float. It was like there were hundreds of tiny bubbles bouncing around in there. They **ping-ponged** their way into his chest and **bing-bonged** their way up into his throat. And then . . .

B-U-U-U-R-P!

George let out a big burp. A *huge* burp. A SUPER burp!

The super burp was loud, and it was *magic*.

Suddenly George lost control of his arms and legs. It was like they had minds of their own. His hands grabbed straws and stuck them up his nose **like a walrus**. His feet jumped up on the table and he started dancing the hokey-pokey. Everyone at the ice cream parlor started laughing— **except George's parents**, who were covered in ice cream from the sundaes he had knocked over.

That wasn't the only time the super burp had **burst** its way out of George's belly. There had been plenty of magic gas attacks since then. And every time the burp came, trouble followed. George never knew when a burp  would strike or what it would make him do. Like juggle raw eggs in his classroom (which **would have been fine** if George actually knew *how* to juggle).

The super burps even followed George to the fourth-grade field day. One burp made George bark like a dog and lick the principal's hand.

The last thing George wanted was for the super burp to start bubbling over on Louie's birthday. George didn't know what Louie would do if George ruined his party.

And **he didn't really want to find out**.

Chapter 2

"Hi, George. Where are you going?" George's best friend Alex asked him when the boys ran into each other near the park later that Saturday morning.

"Mr. Furstman's pet shop," George said. "I promised I'd be there by noon today." George worked at the pet shop every Saturday. He liked being around the animals. George didn't have a pet. His dad was allergic to just about everything but fish. And fish didn't really count as pets.

Alex looked down at his watch. "It's only eleven," he said.

Alex was the only kid George knew who wore a watch. Most kids just stopped some grown-up and asked what time it was—when they even *cared* what time it was.

But **Alex's watch was definitely cool**. It lit up at night, and you could wear it if you went **deep-sea diving**—not that Alex had ever done that. Alex was more the kind of kid who would wear nose plugs to go underwater in the bathtub. Not that Alex wasn't cool. He just wasn't into doing any kind of sporty stuff. He was more **a science and math kind of guy**.

"I'm going in early because I ran out of stuff to do," George said. "And my mom was yelling at me to turn off the TV. What are you up to?"

"Breaking a world record," Alex said.

George stared at him. *What a weird answer.*

"You know, like in the book," Alex explained.

George knew exactly what Alex was talking about: the *Schminess Book of World Records*. It was filled with pictures of people who had broken **all sorts of records** —like being the person with the longest toenails or plucking a turkey the fastest or eating the most cockroaches in one sitting. George had bought the same book at the school bookfair the week before. **Pretty much all the boys had.**

Alex reached into his pocket and pulled out a plastic bag. Inside was a big, round gray blob.

"What's that?" George asked.

"It's the start of **my world**

record-breaking ABC gum ball," Alex explained.

"What's ABC gum?" George asked him.

"Already been chewed," Alex said. "I'm collecting pieces of chewed gum and sticking them together. **The world record is a wad with a four-foot diameter.** It weighs seventy-seven pounds and twelve ounces. I'm going to keep collecting used gum until this ball is even bigger."

"Wow! Go for it, dude!" George said, **high-fiving** Alex. If Alex really *could* break the world record for collecting ABC gum,

WORLD'S LARGEST
ABC GUM WAD!

4 FT

he would get his name and his picture in the *Schminess Book of World Records*. It would be amazing to have a world-famous friend. Almost as amazing as being world-famous himself.

Of course, Alex still had a long way to go. His wad of gum was currently only about the size of a baseball. Still, it must have taken a lot of chewing to even get it to that size.

"You chewed *all* that gum?" George asked.

Alex shook his head. "Nah. Just some of it. **The rest I got other places**—like on the sidewalk or under some desks at school. You'd be surprised where people stick ABC gum. I even found some in a bathroom stall at a diner."

"Come on," George told Alex. He started walking down the street. "Let's hit the newsstand. I'll buy a pack of gum. I'll

chew it up real good and give it all to you."

"You're a good friend, George," Alex said. "Thanks."

"I bet you'll be the **first kid from Beaver Brook** to get in the *Schminess Book of World Records*," George told Alex.

"I don't know," Alex said. "Maybe."

As Alex and George walked to the newsstand, George began to think about what record *he* could break. He didn't want to grow his toenails really long because then he'd have to get all new

shoes, and George hated shoe shopping. And he wasn't sure he wanted to find out what it felt like to have a cockroach crawling down his throat and into his stomach. **He had eaten worms once—the burps made him**—and they hadn't tasted so great.

In fact, the only thing George could think of that could be world record–worthy were his burps. And George didn't want to break that kind of record!

When the boys reached the newsstand,

George counted the change in his pocket to buy **a big pack of Super Bubble Bubble Gum**.

"Dude, there are ten pieces in there," Alex said. "Want me to chew half of them?"

"Sure," George said. He opened the pack of Super Bubble Bubble Gum. Then, suddenly, he felt a fizzy feeling in the bottom of his belly. His eyes **bulged**.

George had felt those fizzies flip-flopping around in his belly before. They could only mean one thing: *The super burp was back, and it wanted to come out and play!*

It had been over a week since his last burp, and it felt like this one was making up for lost time. Already it was ping-ponging its way out of George's belly and bing-bonging its way into his chest.

This could be really *ba-a-ad*!

George had to squelch the belch. Fast! So **he did the first thing that popped into**

his head. He shoved pieces of bubble gum into his mouth and started chewing as fast as he could. Maybe the gum could block the burp and stop it from getting out of his mouth.

"George, you okay?" Alex asked him.

George didn't answer. He shoved in more gum and kept on chewing. But the super burp was powerful. All the gassy air blew straight into the wad of chewed gum. First it was a small bubble. Then a medium-sized bubble. Then a massive, **gigundo-sized** bubble that was as big as George's head.

"Whoa! This could be a record-breaking bubble!" Alex said.

And then . . .

Whoosh! George felt the air rush right out of his belly. It was like someone had popped a bubble gum bubble inside of him. The super burp had disappeared. Hooray!

Pop! Suddenly, the air rushed right out of the massive, gigundo bubble gum bubble. Pieces of bubble gum were stuck all over George's face—his lips, his hair, **even up his nose**.

George picked a huge glob of gum out of his hair and held it out to Alex. "Here. You want this?"

"Um . . . I don't know," Alex said. "I'm not sure if hairy ABC gum counts."

"Yeah," George agreed. He dug his finger up his nose and pulled a glob of gummy, pink gunk from his nostril. "Guess you don't want this, either," he said.

"I better not," Alex answered. "I don't want to take a chance that I could be disqualified."

George had a feeling he was going to be picking gum off his face and hair for the rest of the day. And none of it was going to be part of Alex's ABC gum ball.

What a waste. Stupid super burp.

Chapter 3

On Monday morning, the whole fourth grade was talking about Alex's ABC gum ball.

"I saved you some of my organic spearmint gum," Sage told Alex. She pulled a small plastic bag out of her backpack. "The minute George told me what you were doing, I wanted to help."

Alex shot George a strange look because it was hard to believe that George would tell Sage anything. Sage had a crush on George. **She made him crazy.**

"She was in the pet store buying bird food and heard me telling Mr. Furstman about you," George explained to Alex. "I was talking about the ABC gum ball with *him*. *She* just overheard."

"So many colorful birds came to the feeder in our yard this weekend," Sage told George. She batted her eyelashes up and down and gave him a **big smile**. "You recommended just the right stuff."

George shrugged. "It's the only birdseed Mr. Furstman sells."

"Well, it was still perfect," Sage said.

"I've got three globs of gum for you," Chris told Alex. "My mom said it was gross to save ABC gum, so I kept them under my bed. But **don't worry, I pulled off all the dust bunnies**."

"Thanks," Alex said. He took the globs of gum and stuck them onto his ball.

George was impressed. The ABC

gum ball was definitely bigger. Alex
had added **a lot of gum** since Saturday
morning.

Just then, Louie strutted onto the
playground. His friends, Mike and Max,
were right behind him—like always.
George called them the Echoes.

"I bet you guys are all deciding what
to get me for my birthday," Louie said.
"Don't stop talking just because I'm here.
I already know what's on the list."

"He knows because he wrote the list," Mike said.

"It's a great list," Max added.

Louie smiled. "I hope someone gets me the night-vision goggles," he said. "And I'd really like that **portable popcorn maker**. It's the third item down on my list. You can't miss it."

"Actually, we're talking about Alex," George told Louie. "He's going to break a world record."

"For what? Having the geekiest friends?" Louie asked.

Mike and Max both laughed.

"At least Alex *has* friends," George said.

Mike and Max stopped laughing.

"Louie has friends," Max said.

"Yeah," Mike added. "What are we?"

George started laughing. **"You don't really want me to answer that, do you?"**

Just then, Julianna came over. She walked right past Louie and started talking to Alex. "I want to interview you for my sportscast this morning."

"Why him?" Louie asked. "Alex stinks at sports."

Edith B. Sugarman Elementary School had its own TV station—WEBS TV. Julianna was **the fourth grade's sportscaster**.

"I want to interview Alex about his ABC gum ball," Julianna explained.

"Since when is collecting used gum a sport?" Louie asked.

"Going for a world record means you are competing for a title," Julianna explained. "And sports are all about competition."

George grinned. She had Louie there.

"Alex, now everyone in the school is going to hear about your ABC gum ball," George said. "They're all going to give you their used gum. You'll break the record in no time!"

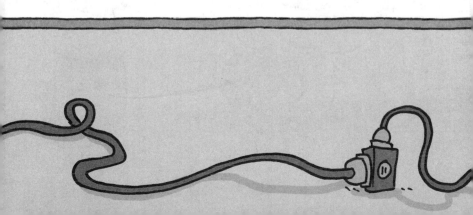

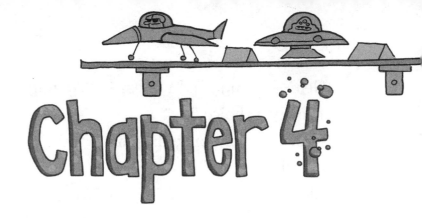

Chapter 4

Even though Louie was a jerk, George still had to buy him a birthday present. So George and his mother went to Tyler's Toy Shop right after school. Alex came with them.

"Louie's list is really long," Alex said. **He held up the two-page printout** Mr. Tyler had given them. "How many presents does he think he's going to get?"

George shrugged. "I guess he's giving everybody a choice."

George's mom picked up an art kit. "What about this?"

Alex shook his head. "Nope. Not on the list."

George stopped in front of a purple-and-green striped basketball. "Is this on the list?"

Alex nodded.

"Maybe I'll get it," George said.

Alex thought for a second. "Bad move," he said. "Louie will use it for **killer ball**. Basketballs are really hard. And that game hurts enough already."

No kidding. Killer ball was a game Louie made up. It was a lot like dodgeball, only meaner. "So what about a deluxe rocket kit?" George said. He picked up the box and read the back. "It says that it is air-powered and can shoot up to two hundred feet in the air."

George's mom looked at the price tag. "It's awfully expensive."

"What if we split it?" Alex suggested.

Before George could ask his mom, he suddenly felt something strange brewing way down in his belly. It was fizzing and whizzing around.

George knew that what he was dealing with wasn't air powered. **It was *gas* powered.** And no way was it on Louie's list.

The super burp was back! Already it had ping-ponged its way out of George's belly and was bing-bonging up into his chest.

The burp was ready to blast off. And this time it was not going to be stopped. Before George could do anything, the burp ping-ponged right up George's throat, zigzagged its way between his teeth, made its way to his lips, and . . .

"George!" his mom shouted.

"Whoa, dude!" Alex said.

It was the loudest burp anyone had ever heard. It practically broke the sound barrier. Alex was covering both his ears.

Suddenly, George felt his feet running over to the bikes in the back of the store.

"Where are you going?" he heard his mom call.

He wasn't making his feet move. They were doing it all on their own. **It was like George was an old-fashioned puppet and someone else was pulling the strings.** He was heading to the bicycle aisle in the store.

George felt his rear end land—*thud!*—on the seat of a little red-and-white tricycle. The next thing he knew, he was pedaling the trike all around the store.

"*Wheeeeee!*" George shouted.

George didn't want to ride a baby bike. He really didn't. But George wasn't in the driver's seat now. The burp was.

"George!" his mother shouted. "Get off that, *now*."

Alex was shaking his head and laughing.

George wanted to get off the tricycle.

But his rear end didn't. It felt like it was superglued to the seat.

"*Whee!* Here I come!" George shouted.

Honk! Honk! Suddenly, George's hands began squeezing the big horn on the handlebars. *Honk! Honk!*

"Young man!" a woman in a green floppy hat cried as she leaped out of the way. "You almost ran over my foot!"

"Stop that at once!" Mr. Tyler shouted at George.

Instead, George rode around the lady in a circle. "Beep! Beep! Watch out! I just got my driver's license."

"I'll get my son's birthday gifts another time," the woman with the green floppy hat told Mr. Tyler. **"It's dangerous in here."** Then she raced out of the shop.

"You're scaring away the customers!" Mr. Tyler shouted at George.

The tricycle had now reached the front of the toy store. George's butt

suddenly got unstuck from the tricycle seat. His legs jumped off the trike. George waited to hear the *whoosh* sound that meant the burp was over. But it didn't come. The next thing he knew, George was climbing into the storefront window where there was a huge display of wooden paddleball toys.

George's hands grabbed two paddleball toys. His hands started paddling the balls between George's legs and over his head. They paddled front. They paddled back. George had never been very good at this before. **But now he was a whiz**.

People walking outside on the street stopped to watch him.

The crowd outside was growing. A few little kids were cheering. **The yellow-haired woman in the green sun hat** was staring at George now. She looked so shocked that her eyes were bugging right out of her head.

"George!" Alex shouted. "Are you going for the world paddling record?"

"No. He's not," George's mom said. "GEORGE! Stop that!"

But George's hands kept paddling. They paddled up. They paddled down. They . . . *CRASH!* They paddled right into the display of paddleball toys and knocked it to ground.

Whoosh! Just then **George felt something go pop** in the bottom of his belly. It was like the air just rushed out of him.

The super burp was gone.

George was sitting in the middle of a pile of paddleball toys. He opened his mouth to say, "I'm sorry." And that's exactly what came out.

Mr. Tyler was really angry. "Sorry doesn't fix my display, young man," he told George. "You need to leave. Right now."

"But I haven't bought a gift yet," George said.

"You'd better take your business somewhere else," Mr. Tyler told George's mom. He looked down at George and **frowned**. "*Anywhere* else."

Chapter 5

"So, what are you going to do about a present for Louie?" Alex asked George the next day after school. The boys were hanging out in Alex's backyard.

Alex was staring at George in a weird way. It was like he was trying to figure something out, but he couldn't. It made George feel like **he was a puzzle with a missing piece**. It wasn't a very good feeling.

"I got him a
rock music CD,"
George said. "I
had to wait in
the car while my
mom went into
the music store
to buy it."

"Probably safer that way," Alex said.
Alex stood there for a minute. Then, finally,
he said, "Ummmm. Look, dude, **did you
ever notice** that whenever you let out a
massive burp, you get all weird and wacky?"

"What—what do you mean?" George
stuttered.

"You know what I mean," Alex said.
"It's like something comes over you, and
you go nuts."

George gulped. It was no use pretending
nothing was wrong. Alex had figured it out.
Sort of. Maybe Alex would understand. "It's

not my fault," George said. "I get . . ."

Oh man. How was George supposed to talk about his super burps? **It would sound crazy.** It *was* crazy!

"You're going to think I'm nuts," George said slowly. "But right after I moved here . . ." George took a deep breath. "Okay, here goes," he said. "My burps aren't normal burps. They're *magic.*"

"There's no such thing as magic," Alex told him.

"Yeah, that's what I always thought, too," George said. "But my burps really are magic."

George could tell by the way Alex was wrinkling his forehead that he didn't believe him. It wasn't going to be easy to get a science guy like Alex to believe in magic.

"Are you talking about magic, like a magic trick?" Alex asked.

"No. *Magic* magic. Not trick magic," George told him. George knew all about magic tricks—he put on shows for his parents all the time. **He was the Great Georgini.** But this was different. "Whenever I have a magic burp, it takes over and makes me do stuff

I don't want to do. Like yesterday at the toy store. The magic burp made me get on that trike."

"You're serious? You're not kidding me?" Alex stared so hard at George it was like he were peering into his brain. It was the same look George's mom had given him that time she tried to figure out who broke her lamp.

George raised both his hands. "Dude, this is the truth."

"So when you exploded the volcano while we were showing our science project . . . ," Alex began.

"The magic burp," George said.

"And when you jumped off the trampoline and got your underpants stuck on the tree branch—"

"With the world's worst wedgie? **Yeah**, that was the burp, too."

"And when you juggled raw eggs, went

after the skunk, and dive-bombed into the principal's lap?"

"Burp. Burp. And more burp," George said.

Alex sat on the ground. **He blinked a few times.** George could see he was trying to wrap his mind around something big—even bigger than the world's biggest wad of gum.

"Wow. Magic burps," Alex said finally. "When did it start?"

"Just a few weeks ago. I was normal before. I swear," George said. "I had a root beer float at Ernie's, and the first one came right after that."

Alex thought about that for a minute.

"There's got to be a cure. But it's going to take a lot of hard work before we find it, that's for sure," he said.

"We?" George asked. "You're going to help me?"

Alex nodded. "Sure. I don't want you to keep getting in trouble."

"Neither do I," George said. He stopped for a minute. "You won't tell anybody, will you? My parents don't even know."

"Your secret is safe," Alex promised.

"You can't even tell Chris," George went on. Chris was George's second best friend in Beaver Brook. "The fewer people who know about this the better."

George smacked himself in the forehead. "Can you imagine if Louie found out?"

"Yeah, that would be bad," Alex agreed. "He'd never stop making fun of you."

"No kidding," George said. "He'd

probably stop calling me New Kid and start calling me Gassy Guy."

Alex thought for a minute. "Tell me again about the first burp?" he asked.

"It happened at Ernie's," George said. "It was right after I drank a root beer float. But I've had **thousands of root beer floats** in my life. This time, though, a shooting star went by, and I made a wish. I think the wish came true but got kind of mixed up."

"And that's what made the magic burps come?" Alex had an "I don't think so" look on his face.

"Yeah," George said.

"Then we need to go back to Ernie's," Alex said.

"No way," George said. "I did the hokey-pokey on a table with straws up my nose the last time I was there."

"We need to check out the scene of the

burp if we're going to find a cure," Alex insisted.

George folded his hands in front of chest. "Uh-uh."

"How about if you wear a disguise?" Alex suggested.

George thought about that for a minute. **"It would have to be a really good disguise."**

Chapter 6

"I better not run into the waitress who served me that root beer float," George said. He felt **sick to his stomach** as they rounded the corner.

"She'll never recognize you," Alex said. George was wearing a baseball cap pulled low over his eyes and a pair of glasses with a fake nose and moustache attached.

They were standing in front of Ernie's.

"Which table were you at?" Alex asked. "We have to sit at the exact same one."

"Outside. Third one from the left," George said.

Alex and George sat down at the table. **A waiter skated over.** "Hi, guys," he said.

"Hi," Alex answered.

"Hello," George said. He tried to disguise his voice so he sounded older.

"Nice 'stache," the waiter said.

"Thanks," George said.

"What are you having?" the waiter asked Alex.

"I'll have a vanilla and chocolate swirly cone," Alex told him.

"And for you, sir?" The waiter turned to George.

"He'll have a root beer float."

"*Ummm* . . . I don't know about that," George said nervously.

"You have to," Alex said under his breath. "We have to figure out what made the *you-know-what* happen."

"Okay," George said. "A root beer float."

"I'll be right back with your orders," the waiter told them as he skated off.

George looked around. "I don't know what you think we're going to find out here."

"I'm not sure," Alex admitted. "But **scientists always replicate** their experiments to see if the same thing happens again."

"Repli-what?" George asked him.

"Repli*cate*," Alex repeated. "It means do something over and over again. So you have to drink a root beer float over again, just the way you did before. We can see if the burp shows up and makes you act weird. Maybe it's **an allergic reaction** to the root beer they serve."

George still wasn't sure. But at least this experiment involved drinking a root beer float. **That used to be his favorite thing in the world.** But he hadn't had one since that bad, *ba-a-ad* night.

While waiting for their order, George reached under the table. "Hey, check it out!" he shouted. He held up a hardened piece of gum. "ABC gum!"

"Awesome," Alex said. He took the gum from George and squished it onto his **ever-growing gum ball**. It was so large now, it bulged out of Alex's backpack.

George reached underneath his chair. There was a piece of gum there, too. "Here's some more," he said excitedly.

"That one's still a little gooey," Alex said. "Must have been just been chewed."

A minute later, Alex's ice cream and George's root beer float arrived.

"Here you go," the waiter said as he placed them on the table. "Enjoy!"

George stared at the root beer float with its scoop of ice cream and whipped cream topping. **It looked so innocent!** But what if the fizzy bing-bonging and ping-ponging started up again?

Alex was examining the root beer float, too. "You know, it looks like they use extra bubbly root beer," he said. "And maybe it's the bubbles in the soda that make you burp."

"Yeah, but even if the root beer has extra strong bubbles, why would they make me do crazy stuff?" George pointed out.

"That's true," Alex said with a shrug. "But we have to start our experiment somewhere. **Drink up!**"

George put his mouth around the straw.

"Wait!" Alex shouted.

George popped the straw right out of his mouth. "What?"

"You have to drink it *exactly* the same way you drank the float that gave you the burp," Alex said. "Otherwise we are not replicating the experiment. Did you drink it fast or slow?"

"Fast," George said. "*Really* fast. I was thirsty."

Alex looked down at his watch. "Okay, go ahead and drink. I'll time how long it takes you."

"Why?" George asked.

"Because we need all the data we

can collect," Alex said. "That's the scientific way!" He looked at his watch. "On your mark. Get set. Go!"

Slurp. The creamy root beer went through the straw, into George's mouth, and **down into his belly**.

And then he waited for something *ba-a-ad* to happen.

He waited.
And waited.
And waited. But nothing happened.

"Maybe you have to drink it faster,"

Alex suggested. "Forget the straw."

George picked up the glass and took a huge gulp.

Alex started to laugh.

George stopped slurping and looked up. He hadn't felt any fizzing. He hadn't let out so much as a **mini burp**. And he certainly wasn't dancing on tables or doing anything else weird.

"What's so funny?" George asked.

"Your moustache," Alex said. He pointed to the root beer float.

George looked down. The moustache was floating on top of the drink. It looked like **a big, hairy spider floating on a mountain of ice cream**.

58

George took the moustache out of the glass. He licked all the ice cream off the ends. No point in wasting perfectly good ice cream. Then he finished the float while Alex sucked the last of his ice cream out of the bottom of his cone.

Alex made George wait fifteen minutes to see if a burp came.

Nothing. Absolutely nothing.

By the time the boys finally left Ernie's, Alex had fourteen new wads of ABC gum stuck on his gum ball. But they hadn't figured out how to stop the magical super burp.

You couldn't find the cure for something like that hidden under a tabletop. Super burps were *w-a-a-ay* **too sneaky for that**.

Chapter 7

By the time Louie's birthday party rolled around, George had been **burp-free for four days**. Alex thought maybe drinking the root beer float at Ernie's had cured George. But he wasn't taking any chances.

One day Alex had said, "I have been doing some research. We need to improve your digestion." So he made George curl up in a ball with his legs tucked into his chest and roll around and around, because Alex read somewhere that rolling around makes stomach gas go away.

Another day, Alex had George breathe into a paper bag three times after every meal.

On the other two days, Alex made George do **one hundred sit-ups** to keep his stomach strong so his muscles could hold down the burp. Just in case.

George did what Alex said, but he was scared the magic burps were just lying in wait, ready to pop out at the worst time—like right in the middle of Louie's party.

"I will not burp. I will not burp," George said over and over to himself as he walked to Alex's house on Saturday morning. George's mom had to work at her shop, the Knit Wit craft store, and his dad was at the army base before George even woke up. So Alex's mom was driving them to the party.

"I will not burp. I will not burp," George said again as he rang the doorbell to Alex's house.

"Hi. How does it feel to go ninety-six hours without a single burp?" Alex asked as he opened the door.

"*Shhhhh!*" George said. **He looked around nervously.**

"Relax," Alex said. "My mom's in the laundry room. You can't hear anything over that clunky dryer. And Chris won't be here for fifteen minutes."

George frowned. He felt bad leaving Chris out of his secret, but if Alex really did find a permanent cure soon, there wouldn't be any burping secret to hide anymore.

"I've been doing more research about burping," Alex told George. "Burps are actually caused by gas."

"Tell me something I don't already know," George said. "I feel fizzy gas all the time."

"Yeah, but did you know that the

gas is made in your stomach and your intestines when your body breaks down food into energy?" Alex asked him.

George started laughing.

"What's so funny?" Alex asked.

"Intestines," George said. "It's a funny word."

"Now listen, you can't eat anything at the party," Alex said. "No food. No burp. **Simple.**"

It did sound simple. Except for one thing: It was a party, and a party meant pizza and birthday cake.

But George would give them up if that was the way to keep Pirate Island a belch-free zone.

The banner for Louie's birthday was the first thing George saw when he, Alex, and Chris entered Pirate Island Water Park later that morning. There was no way anyone could miss it. Alex's mom told the man at the ticket stand that the boys were part of the birthday party. Then they each held out their hand to get **stamped with an image of a pirate's head**.

"This place is the best," Chris said. "The Barracuda Blast log flume is awesome. My little brother threw up on it!"

PIRATE

"Drop your loot right in here," Louie said with a smile.

Louie was standing right inside the entrance wearing a giant pirate hat. Max and Mike were standing beside him holding a large laundry bag.

"*Loot* is pirate talk for presents," Max said.

"Yeah," Mike added. "Pirates have their own talk."

LOOT

ISLAND

RTHDAY,
E!

Duh, George thought to himself as he put his CD into the bag with the rest of gifts. But he didn't say that. He was being the new, well-behaved George. **Even at the water park.**

"Oh, and there's no gum-chewing in the water park," Louie said. "That means you can't work on breaking your world record today." He gave Alex a nasty grin.

Alex shrugged. "That's okay. I got time."

"This is going to be the best party ever," Louie said. "You can go anywhere you want in the whole park."

Wow! George liked the sound of that.

"Of course, I'm the only one with a golden ticket. My parents paid a whole lot extra. **Like fifty bucks or something.** But it means I automatically go to the front of the line on any ride," Louie continued. He shoved the plastic card that hung from

a rope around his neck in George's face. "You guys all have to wait in line."

Then Louie passed out a map to each of the guests. The map showed pictures of all the attractions in the park. There was a **giant waterslide** nearby and a log flume right next to it. The map also showed three wild water coasters, a rope swing over a river, and a long, rambling creek that circled the whole park.

"Hey, Ma, hurry up!" Louie started yelling. "Everybody's here."

"I'm coming, Loo Loo Poo," Louie's mom shouted.

George turned and spotted a woman rushing over to them. She was balancing trays with paper cones of cotton candy stuck upright.

The woman had yellow hair, and she was wearing a big green sun hat. **There was something familiar about her.**

Oh man. It was the lady who been in Tyler's Toy Shop the day George had had that major burp attack. *Gulp.* **Quickly** George turned his back to her.

"Ma!" Louie grumbled. "I said to hurry up! I want my cotton candy. Did you get me a purple one?"

Oh no! The woman in the hat was Louie's mom! *Double gulp.*

"It's right here, Loo Loo," she said. "And it's the only purple one. **The birthday boy's cotton candy has to be special.**"

Suddenly Louie's mom stopped in her tracks and took a good, hard look at George. **"Don't I know you?"** she asked.

Triple gulp. "Me? No, no. I'm new in town," George said.

Louie's mom continued staring. "Now I recognize you! You're that crazy kid from the toy store. The one who

practically ran me
over. Aren't you
a little old for a
tricycle?"

Busted.

"I'm going to
keep an eye on
you," she told
him.

*I will not
burp . . . I
will not
burp . . .*
George
kept telling himself as **his hand shot out
toward the tray of cotton candy cones.**
But Alex grabbed him before he took one.

"No way, dude," Alex whispered
inGeorge's ear. "Cotton candy is a burp
waiting to happen."

"Oh, right," George said unhappily.

He put his hand down and said **"no thanks"** to Louie's mom.

"Don't you like cotton candy, George?" Sage asked him.

George shook his head. "I don't want to go in the water right after eating. I could . . . uh . . . get a cramp or something."

"You're not going swimming," Louie said. "It's just a slide."

"Sliding," Max said.

"Not swimming," Mike added.

"I heard him the first time," George told Mike and Max. He really had to get out of there. Louie's whole mouth was turning **bright purple** from his cotton candy. It was making George *sooo* hungry.

"Okay, kids," Louie's mom told everyone. "You are free to walk around the park by yourselves and go on any ride you like."

"You guys ready to go on the H2-Oh No

slide?" George asked Chris and Alex.

"Yeah!" Chris and Alex said at the same time.

"Then come on," George said.

"Wait up!" Sage shouted after the boys. "I want to go on the H2-Oh No slide with you!"

Oh man. Was Sage going to be following George around all day long?

"It's a really big slide," George told her. "And it goes really fast."

"That's okay," Sage said, hurrying to keep up as George and his friends raced to the H2-Oh No slide. There was already a big line. Sage stood beside George and smiled in a way that **made him kind of sick to his stomach**.

"You're so brave, George. I bet you're not scared to go on anything! I'll close my eyes and hold on to you. I know you'll keep me safe."

George pretended
not to hear. And
he pretended not to
notice Alex, Chris, and Sage
finishing their cotton candy.
Instead, he waited patiently as
the line snaked up the stairs to the
top of the slide. He was thinking
about how far up he was and how
fun this ride was going to be.

It was a four-lane slide.
**Each path looped around in a
different, crazy direction.**

At the very top, George,
Alex, Chris, and Sage lay down
on their backs. Sage reached for
George's hand.

George did NOT reach
back. Sage was going to have
to **go it alone**.

"Ready?" the pirate at

the top of the slide asked.

"Oh yeah!" George cheered. He was totally ready to slide down the H2-Oh No. **This was gonna be fu-u-un!**

Wheee! The next thing George knew, he was zooming down the slide. Water was splashing all around him. He was zooming over bumps and zigzagging around turns.

"AWESOME!" George shouted out, although nobody could hear him. **He closed his eyes.** It made the ride even scarier!

Splash! George landed in the big pool of water at the bottom of the H2-Oh No slide.

Splash! Alex plunged into the pool right behind George.

Splash! Down came Chris.

Splash! Sage landed last.

"Yo, Sage, your face is green," George told her as they all climbed out of the pool at the end of the plunge and returned their mats.

Sage didn't answer for a moment. Then she said, **"I think I just threw up a little in my mouth."**

"Cool," Chris said.

"Want to go down again?" Alex asked.

"Maybe let's go for a water coaster." Chris answered.

"Yeah!" George cheered. "How about the one that turns upside-down in the middle?"

Now Sage looked **really** green. "I think I'll go to the arcade. I need to stay on dry land for a while."

"Okay, see you later," George said happily. As she walked away, he added, "All it took to get rid of Sage was a little ABS cotton candy"

"ABS?" Alex asked. "What's that?"

"Already been swallowed," George said. "And then it got thrown up and swallowed a second time."

"Gross, dude," Alex said. But he was laughing, too.

Chapter 8

"Louie, Louie . . . Aye yi yi yi."

The words to the classic rock song blared out from the speakers all around the water park. No way was George—or anybody else—going to forget that it was Louie's birthday.

And then there were the posters. They were everywhere, too. As George, Alex, and Chris floated in their inner tubes around another turn in Castaway Creek,

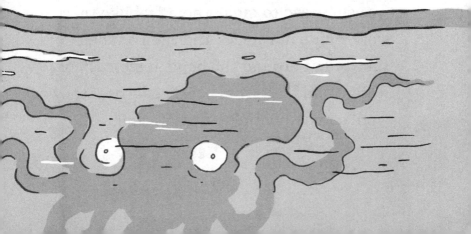

there was Louie's big, goofy face on a poster, saying, *Have You Seen This Guy? If You Do, Wish Him a Happy Birthday!*

HAVE YOU
SEEN THIS GUY?

IF YOU DO, WISH HIM
A HAPPY BIRTHDAY!

Still, George and his pals were having a great time. It was sunny and hot—but not too hot. They were all sitting in their own **bright orange inner tubes**, riding around in a shallow stream of blue water.

Every now and then, the water would start bubbling beneath their rear ends—**on purpose!** It was supposed to make them feel like they were riding in rapids. And then as their tubes went around the bend, a big rush of water would fall from overhead—as if they were going under a giant waterfall.

"Glub! Glub! Glub!" Chris shouted as he opened his mouth and swallowed water from the waterfall.

That looked like fun. George started to open his mouth, too. Suddenly, he got a fizzy feeling in his gut.

George shut his mouth quickly.

Oh no! There was no way. George hadn't had anything to eat or drink. No cotton candy. No root beer. So this couldn't be the super burp.

Or could it? Already bubbles were bouncing around like crazy inside him. Oh yeah! It was **definitely** the super burp. And it wanted out. NOW!

George's eyes opened wide. He waved his arms in Alex's direction, trying to get his buddy's attention. Alex had to help him keep the burp from bursting.

But Alex was too busy paddling his way over toward a pirate cannon on the side of the creek that was shooting cold water at people.

Bing-bong. Ping-pong. The burp was up in George's mouth now. It was zigzagging its way between his teeth and over his tongue.

All of a sudden, Alex spun around. **He'd heard what happened** and started paddling frantically toward George.

Too late. George had already let out a burp so loud it drowned out "Louie Louie" on the loudspeakers.

George opened his mouth to say, "Excuse me." But that's not what came out. Instead, George's mouth shouted, "SHARK!"

Everyone turned to stare at him. One little kid, who was sharing a double tube with his dad, burst out crying.

The burp was in control now. George's legs leaped from his inner tube.

"Dude, no!" Alex shouted.

The lifeguards began blowing their whistles. But if George's ears heard the whistles, they weren't listening. His body was way too busy playing shark attack in Castaway Creek.

George's body dived underwater. He swam underneath Chris's inner tube. Then his fingers pinched Chris's rear end.

George's head popped up from under the water. "Shark attack!" he shouted at Chris.

The lifeguards blew their whistles again. One was shouting through a megaphone, "No fooling around in the water. Stop this instant!"

George the shark wasn't going to stop attacking. He swam around, ducking underwater and pinching rear ends.

"Ouch!" a huge man shouted.

"Shark attack!" George's mouth shouted back.

"Somebody do something about this kid!" a woman in a flowery bathing cap called to the lifeguards.

Suddenly, four lifeguards jumped into the shallow water. They started running toward George.

George's eyes looked left.

His eyes looked right.

There were lifeguards coming from every direction. There was no way out.

And then . . .

Whoosh! Suddenly, George felt something pop in his stomach, like someone had punctured a balloon. All the air rushed out of him. The super burp was gone!

But George was still standing in Castaway Creek. He was surrounded by **angry lifeguards and furious people** in inner tubes.

"Get out of the water—now!" one of the lifeguards told him.

George lowered his head. He grabbed his empty inner tube and climbed out of the creek.

Alex got out, too. He shouted to Chris that they'd meet up with him later.

"Now you see what I'm up against," George said.

"You ate something didn't you?" Alex asked as they returned the tires. **"Come on. Admit it."**

"No! I haven't eaten a thing since we got here," George said.

"It could have been your breakfast,"

Alex said. "Delayed reaction."

They turned a corner to return their tubes, and there was Louie.

"I knew it! **I knew it had to be you!** You're trying to ruin my party!" Louie was screaming so loud his face was turning red.

Louie was standing right next to a poster of himself. A little girl looked at the poster, then at Louie and said, "Hey, happy birthday!"

Louie's face got even redder. "Ma!" he shouted across the creek. "Over here! Now! He's doing it again!"

Louie's mom was in an inner tube in the middle of the creek. At the sound of Louie's voice, she leaped out of her tube and ran through the water, pushing people out of the way with every turn until she reached the exit.

"One more stunt like that, and I'm sending you home," Louie's mom scolded

George. "You're not ruining my darling boy's birthday!"

"So much for the not eating thing," George whispered to Alex a little later.

"I was so sure it would work," Alex said.

"I told you, this is no ordinary burp," George told him.

"No kidding," Alex said. "The burp lasted twenty-two seconds. **I timed it on my watch!**"

"Now do you believe it's magic?" George asked. "It's going to take a lot more than not eating to squelch *these* belches."

"There has to be a scientific reason," Alex insisted. "We just need more time. Some scientists take years to figure stuff out."

Years? **That was way too long.** George didn't want to be burping his way through *college*.

They stopped talking because Chris had just come out of the bathroom and saw them. "Hey, look what I found on the paper towel dispenser," he told Alex. "A big wad of ABC gum."

"I thought people weren't allowed to chew gum here," George said.

"I guess somebody needed to get rid of it," Alex said. He took the wad from Chris.

"Where are you going to keep it?" Chris said.

Alex bent down and stuck the gum to the bottom of his flip-flop. "It'll be safe there."

"So, you guys ready for the Stingray Slam?" Chris asked. "I know I am." Then he looked at George and **shook his head in admiration**. "That shark attack was so funny. Dude, you had me laughing so hard, I swallowed water and started choking."

George didn't answer. It hadn't seemed as funny to him.

Alex checked his map. "The Stingray Slam's not far from here. The line's going to be long. But it sounds like it's worth waiting for." Alex read aloud the description. The Stingray Slam was a way-cool water coaster with lots of twists and turns. But the best part came at the end—a final drop that was three stories tall! You had to be **fifty-one inches** to ride on it. George would just make it!

He only hoped he could leave the super burp behind.

Chapter 9

"This ride was amazing. I've been on it twice already," Julianna told George, Chris, and Alex as the boys approached the Stingray Slam. "You're going to get soaked." **She shook her wet hair.** Water dripped all over George and his friends.

"Whoa! Check it out!" Chris exclaimed.

The Stingray Slam was definitely impressive.

It looked like a regular roller coaster with **cars that looked like manta rays**. But the tracks were all filled with water. Lots of water.

George looked over to his left. There was another poster with Louie's goofy, smiling face on it.

But on this one, somebody had drawn **bunny ears and a moustache** on Louie's face. *Hilarious!*

HAVE YOU SEEN THIS GUY?

IF YOU DO, WISH HIM A HAPPY BIRTHDAY!

"Who did you go on the Stingray Slam with?" Alex asked Julianna.

"Sage was supposed to go with me," Julianna explained. "But when we got to the front of the line, **she wimped out.**"

"You want to do it again with us?" he asked her.

"Sure," Julianna said. "I'd go on this a million times."

A few moments later, George, Alex, Julianna, and Chris were ready to get into the first car of the Stingray Slam. Each car had fins on the sides that looked like manta ray fins.

George was so excited, he didn't even care that at the last minute **Louie flashed his golden pass** so that he, Max, and Mike could push ahead of them in line. They piled into the first car.

George and his pals got into the next car. Everyone waited until all the cars were filled.

"Let's get going!" Louie shouted at the guy running the ride.

"I'm not so sure about this," Max said, looking at the drop.

"Me either," Mike added.

"Yes, you are," Louie told them. "You guys are totally psyched."

"Oh, yeah, right," Max said. "I'm psyched."

"Me too," Mike agreed. "I was so psyched I forgot I was psyched."

"All right, everybody, hold on tight," the guy running the ride said.

And **they were off**!

The water coaster boat started out slowly, climbing up, up, up through the river of water. Then without any warning, it twisted to the right.

Splash! A big shower of water came sloshing into the boat. It hit George in the face.

"Oh yeah!" George shouted excitedly. "I didn't see that one coming!"

"Whee!" Everyone shouted as the car tipped over and whooshed around a bend.

In the car ahead, Louie threw his hands up in the air. George started to do that, too. But then, suddenly, he felt a weird fizzy feeling in his belly.

Oh no! **Not again!** It couldn't be. Not the super burp.

But it *was* the super burp. And it was already starting to bing-bong its way out of George's stomach and into his chest.

This just wasn't fair! How many burps could one guy take?

If George started acting all weird, Louie would never let him live it down.

Wait! **Forget Louie.** If the burp came now, who knew what it would make George do? His life might be in danger!

There was no way George was letting this burp burst out. It was a battle between boy and burp. And this time the boy was going to win!

Quickly, George shoved his fist in his

mouth like a stopper in a bottle. The
burp pushed against his fingers. It really
wanted to come out.

"Here comes the drop!" Louie
shouted. He raised his arms way up in
the air.

"*WHOOAAAA!!!*" everyone
shouted.

George kept his fist shoved
in his mouth. His stomach
went up. It went
down. The burp
pushed harder and
harder against his fist.

Splash! As the car
hit the water below,
a huge wave of
water washed over George
and his friends. And then . . .

Whoosh! Suddenly, George felt
something pop in his stomach like

someone had stuck a pin into a balloon.
All the air just rushed out of him. Yay!
George had squelched the belch!

"That was so much fun!" Alex said as
they climbed out of their manta ray cars.

"Wait until you see the pictures,"
Julianna told him.

"What pictures?" Chris asked.

"Didn't you see **that flash** as we hit
the big drop?" Louie asked. "There was
a camera. When we get to the end of
this ramp, the photo will be up on a big
screen. I can't wait to see mine. I had my
hands in the air the whole time."

As they got closer to the ramp, George
heard one kid saying, "Look at that guy."

"Must be talking about me," Louie
said. "I bet I'm the only kid in the world
brave enough not to hold on."

"Look, there he is now," the girl said.
She pointed in Louie's direction.

"See?" Louie said.

But the girl ran up to George. **"Make your blowfish face again,"** she asked him.

Huh? What was she talking about?

Then George looked up at the screen. There was the photo of Louie with his hands high in the air. Max was crouched down low in his seat. Mike was covering his eyes.

There were photos of Alex, Julianna, and Chris. They were all holding on tightly to the bars and laughing.

And then there was George, with his fist shoved in his throat and his cheeks puffed out **really wide** while he tried to keep the burp from bursting.

He *did*
look like
a puffy-
cheeked,
buggy-eyed
blowfish.
And the
burp had
stayed right where it
belonged. In George's belly. Now if he
could only keep it there for the rest of
the day.

Chapter 10

"Will all of Louie's birthday guests please report to Barnacle Barnie's Pizzeria. It's time for lunch!"

George's ears perked up when he heard the announcement coming over the loudspeaker. "I'm eating. I don't care what you say," he whispered to Alex.

Alex shrugged. **"Whatever."**

"Why wouldn't you be eating pizza?" Chris asked.

George looked at the ground. He really hated keeping secrets. Especially from a friend. And now he wasn't sure how he was going to explain this.

"George is . . . um . . . He's trying to break a record," Alex said finally.

"What kind of record?" Chris asked.

"For . . . um . . . the person who goes the longest without eating pizza," Alex told him.

Chris shook his head. "What kind of record is that?" he asked. "That's no fun."

"It's a record that's easy to break," George told him. "There's hardly any competition. But I'm too hungry. I bet I could eat a whole pizza right now."

The boys could smell the pizza before they even walked into Barnacle Barnie's. **It was overwhelming.**

"You guys are all wet," Louie said as George, Alex, and Chris walked into the restaurant.

"It's a water park," George reminded him. "People get wet here."

"Which is why we have towels," Louie's

mother told him. She handed each of the boys a bright orange towel that said *Happy Birthday, Louie!* on it. "You can keep them. They're party favors."

George didn't know why anyone would want a towel with Louie's name on it—other than Louie, of course. But he took the towel, anyway.

"And don't drip on my presents," Louie warned.

"Yo, Louie," Mike called out from a table near the front of the restaurant. "Sit with us."

"Yeah," Max added. "We saved you a seat."

As Louie went off to sit with Max and Mike, George sniffed at the air. *Man, that pizza smells good.*

Just then, Louie's mother walked over to George. "Just remember," she said. "I'm watching you."

George frowned. **Grown-ups always seemed to be watching him.**

"Hey, Mom," Louie called. "Should I open my presents now?"

"I'm coming, Louie," his mom called. Before walking away, she turned around. She pointed to her eyes with two fingers. Then she pointed to George.

He knew what that meant. "You're watching me," George muttered under his breath. "I get it."

A waiter had just set a pie down at their table when suddenly George jumped up. He had to get out of Barnacle Barnie's Pizzeria fast. The fizzy feeling was brewing in his belly.

What if a burp exploded right in the middle of Louie's pizza party? That would be *ba-a-ad*!

"I've got to get out of here," George mumbled to his friends. He was afraid to open his mouth too wide. The super burp was already ping-ponging its way out of his belly and bing-bonging up into his ribs.

"Dude, not the **you-know-what**!" Alex cried. "*Again?*"

But it *was* the you-know-what. *Big time.* George leaped out of his chair and ran for the door.

The minute he got outside, George looked around for some place to hide. He didn't want to **freak out** in public again.

There! On his left! A door!

George had no idea where the door led. He didn't really care. Wherever it was, it wasn't Louie's party. Quickly, he turned the knob, walked inside, and . . .

BUUURP!

George let out a super duper, mighty, mega super burp! It was so loud that everyone in the room turned and stared.

About ten little kids were singing happy birthday to **a boy named**

Will. *Uh oh!* George had just walked into another birthday party.

The next thing George knew, his hands grabbed a long, skinny balloon from the table. Then they started swinging the balloon around like a pirate sword!

"Who are you?" a little kid asked.

George opened his mouth to say, "George Brown." But that's not what came out. Instead, his mouth said. "**Ahoy, mateys!** Captain Long *George* Silver has arrived! *Aargh!*"

"You're late. The other pirates are already here," Will, the birthday boy, said. "See?"

George's eyes looked across the table. Sure enough, there were two waiters in pirate costumes.

"Get out of here, kid," one of them said to George.

George wanted to. He really did. But George wasn't in charge now. The super burp was.

One of the waiters tried to push George out of the room. But George's legs weren't going to let that happen. They jumped up and wrapped themselves around the waiter's back.

"Shiver me timbers!" George's mouth shouted out. "I've got me a prisoner!"

George's hands waved his balloon sword in the air.

"He's funny!" Will shouted.

"Aargh!" George screamed.

Suddenly, all the little kids were grabbing balloons and waving them like swords.

"Aargh!" the kids shouted.

"Aargh!" George's mouth answered.

"Please, children, sit down," Will's parents kept saying.

The waiter tried to wiggle George off of his back. But George's legs held tight.

"Get off me!" the waiter shouted.

And amazingly, that's just what George's body did. His legs let go, and George jumped from the waiter's back . . . **onto the table**.

"Yo ho!" George's mouth shouted out. "Take that! And that! And THAT!"

George was having a duel—with an imaginary pirate.

"Get down from there!" the birthday boy's mom yelled at George.

"Out of my way!" George said. "I'm dueling on the poop deck!"

"Poop deck!" Will giggled. "That's funny."

"I need to make a poop," another kid said.

"Yo ho! Yo ho!" George shouted as he dueled his way down the long table. Cups and plates went flying.

"Watch the cake!" the birthday boy's dad shouted. He raced over and grabbed the cake before George could step in it.

Then the two waiters grabbed George.

"Aargh!" George shouted as he was dragged off the table. He waved his balloon sword and . . . *whoosh*! George felt something pop in his belly.

The super burp was gone.

But George was still there. He opened his mouth to say, "I'm sorry." And that's exactly what came out.

"Sorry doesn't cut it, kid," a waiter said.

"Look at this mess," Will's mother said. "What kind of person ruins a four-year-old's birthday?"

A person with a stupid super burp following him everywhere. **That's who.**

"I'm really sorry," George said. "But it wasn't . . ." George shut his mouth. What could he say? It wasn't me? It was the super burp? Nah. That would never work.

"I still gotta poop," one of the little kids said.

"Happy Birthday," George said to Will.

"Thanks," Will said. "You were funny!"

George smiled. At least the super burp hadn't ruined *everything*.

For once.

ENTER IF YOU DARE

YOU MUST BE THIS TALL

Chapter 11

"Yo, where you been?" Chris asked as he and Alex walked out of Barnacle Barnie's a little while later. "You missed lunch."

"I . . . um . . . I had to go to the bathroom," George said. Then he turned to Alex and mouthed the word **burp**.

"We have time for one more ride," Chris said. "You up for the Tunnel of Terror?"

"Definitely," George said. "The map says that it's the scariest water ride in the

whole park. It's not recommended for **children under seven**."

"Yeah, you slide through a tunnel so **it's completely dark inside**. You can't see a thing. You don't know which way you're turning, or when the end of the slide is coming."

"Sounds scary," Alex said. "Let's go!"

"Right behind you!"

ALMO
THER

2 HR
WAIT

NO
GUM

George told him. "I can't wait!"

But they all had to wait. The Tunnel of Terror wasn't just the scariest water slide at Pirate Island, it was also the most popular. And the line was lo-o-ong. But George didn't care. He was going on this ride no matter what!

The boys left their flip-flops in the cubbies at the bottom of the staircase

AHOY SEA DOGS

1 HOUR

that led to the top of the slide. Then **they began their long climb**.

"It sure is hot out here," Chris said. He wiped a big glob of sweat from his forehead.

"How's the ABC gum on the bottom of your flip-flops doing?" George asked Alex.

"I had to get rid of some of it, because it was making my shoes stick to the ground," Alex said. "But **a couple of nice big blobs** are still there. I'm going to be able to add a few layers to the gum ball when I get home."

"Awesome," George said.

"Check it out," Chris said. "We're almost at the top."

George's heart was pumping so hard, he thought it was going to burst out of his chest, slide down the Tunnel of Terror, and explode at the bottom in a bloody mess!

"Yay! We're next," George told his friends.

"NOT SO FAST!"

Just then, Louie, Max, and Mike pushed past them on the staircase. **They hadn't been waiting in line.** But here they were.

"It's my birthday," Louie told George. "And I have a golden ticket! That means I don't have to wait. I can go ahead of you."

"But we've been waiting in line for like half an hour," George said.

"Who cares?" Louie told him. "I've been waiting *all year* for my birthday! And you're lucky you weren't kicked out of the park. So just stuff it."

And with that, he pushed right in front of George. Max and Mike pushed ahead, too.

"Hey! It's not *your* birthday," George told them. "And you don't have golden tickets."

"We're with Louie," Max said.

"Yeah, **we're with Louie**," Mike agreed.

There was no
point in fighting all
three of them. So George
stepped aside.

And then, finally, George
found himself at the top of
the staircase, staring into
**the mouth of the Tunnel of
Terror**. It sure was dark
in there.

"You ready, kid?" the
guy who was in charge of the
ride asked.

"I guess so,"
George answered
nervously.

"Good luck!"
shouted Alex and Chris.

The guy gave George
a shove.

Wheeeee! George went sliding into the darkness.

"Aaaaahhhhh!" George shouted. It was scary in there. **Good-scary,** though. The kind of scary you go to water parks for.

George twisted. He turned. He tried to look around, but he couldn't see a thing. He was going so fast it almost felt like his swimming trunks were being ripped off him.

And then, finally, **he raced out into the daylight** and splashed into a giant pool of water.

Before he could even open his eyes, George heard bells ringing everywhere. Lights started to flash. A woman with a big bunch of balloons raced through the water and came up to him.

"What did I do?" George asked nervously. He hadn't burped. He hadn't belched. He hadn't even sneezed. So what were all these alarms about?

"Congratulations!" The woman with the balloons shouted to George. "You're the **one millionth park guest** to ride the Tunnel of Terror!"

"Wow!" George exclaimed.

"And here's a lifetime free pass to Pirate Island Water Park," she told him.

"No way!" George exclaimed.

"Congratulations," the woman said. "Smile for the camera. You're going to have your picture in the newspaper."

"NOW WAIT JUST A MINUTE!"

Suddenly Louie came racing through the water. "It's *my* birthday! I should be the one getting the lifetime free pass," he said.

"I'm sorry," the lady said. "But this prize is only for the one millionth guest to ride the Tunnel of Terror."

George laughed. If Louie had **just waited** for George, Alex and Chris to go before him, he would have been the one millionth person.

Louie stared at George. "This is all your fault."

"Yeah," Mike and Max said at the exact same time.

"*My* fault?" George looked at Louie. "You're the one who butted in front."

Louie was really mad now. He started jumping up and down and splashing the water all around. "I should be the winner!" he shouted. "It's my birthday!"

By now, a whole crowd had gathered at the bottom of the Tunnel of Terror. They were all staring at Louie, pointing and laughing. George didn't blame them. Louie was the one having a weirdo freak-out now. And **George was a celebrity**.

Of course, that didn't mean the super burp wasn't going to cause more trouble. **George had a feeling** there would be about **a billion** more belches to squelch. But for now, anyway, he was burp-free. And that was a great feeling.

About the Author

Nancy Krulik is the author of more than 150 books for children and young adults including three *New York Times* best sellers and the popular Katie Kazoo, Switcheroo books. She lives in New York City with her family, and many of George Brown's escapades are based on things her own kids have done. (No one delivers a good burp quite like Nancy's son, Ian!) Nancy's favorite thing to do is laugh, which comes in pretty handy when you're trying to write funny books!

About the Illustrator

Aaron Blecha was raised by a school of giant squid in Wisconsin and now lives with his wife in London, England. He works as an artist and animator designing toys, making cartoons, and illustrating books, including the Zombiekins series. You can enjoy more of his weird creations at www.monstersquid.com.